SERGIO

Makes a Splash!

by Edel Rodriguez

LITTLE, BROWN AND COMPANY

Books for Young Readers

New York   Boston

This is Sergio. He has a beak, wings, and a tail, but unlike most birds, he can't fly.

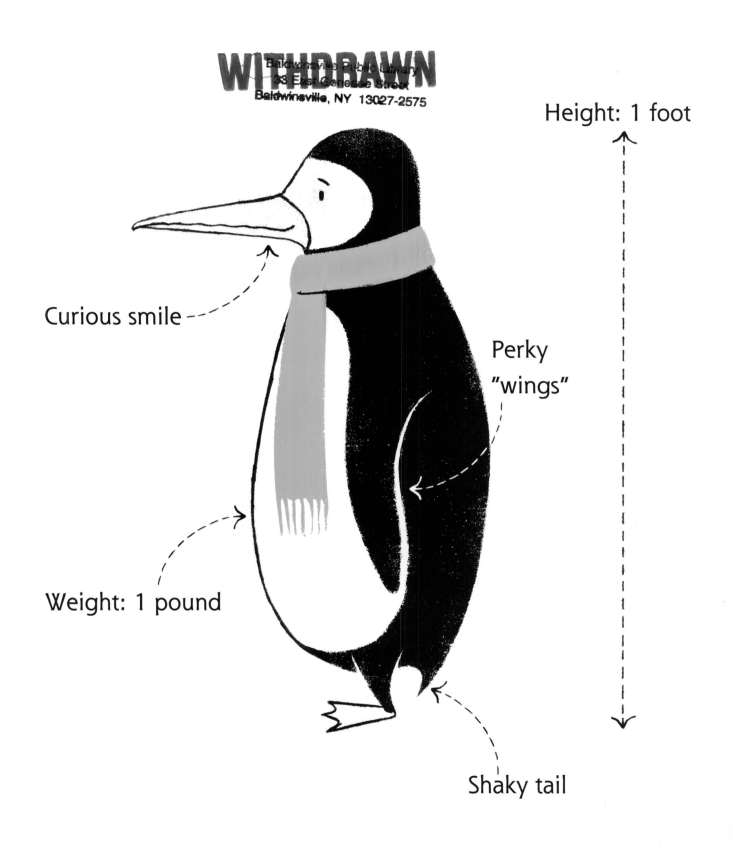

Height: 1 foot

Curious smile

Perky "wings"

Weight: 1 pound

Shaky tail

Sergio is from Argentina,
down by the South Pole,
where it's really cold.

Sergio likes many things,
but the three things he loves
the most are soccer, fishies,
and water.

Especially water.
When he's around water,
Sergio can be:

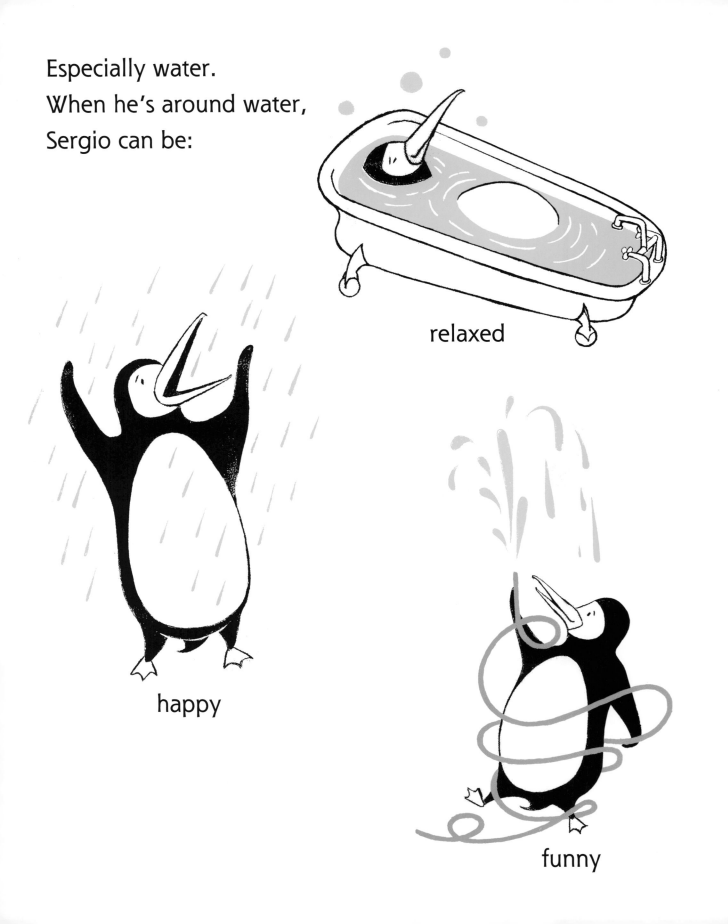

relaxed

happy

funny

playful

and silly

all of which makes him thirsty—for more water, of course!

But sometimes, he can be scared of water,
especially the very deep kind . . .

because Sergio can't swim.

On his first day of school,
Sergio and his classmates
go on a field trip.

The bus stops and everyone hops out.
There is water as far as the eye can see.

Mrs. Waddle tells the class that
they are going to learn how to swim.
Sergio's friends are so excited.
Sergio is not so sure.

The ocean is just like all of those—just a teeny-weeny bit

BIGGER.

And, you know those little fishies you love so much? Where do you think they come from?

It's clear!

I can't swim!

I've got floaties!

. . . and a snorkel . . .

. . . and a life preserver.

One by one,
all of Sergio's friends
begin jumping into
the vast ocean below.

Maybe it will be like taking a bath after all.
He hops to the edge, closes his eyes . . .

And jumps!
But his aim is a bit off.

Sergio plops into the water with a BIG SPLASH and disappears into the darkness.

Sergio's friends
and Mrs. Waddle
watch and wait.

Suddenly there is another
BIG SPLASH and Sergio
pops out of the water!

On the way back to school, Sergio is tired but happy.

"That was better than the rain, puddles, and a cold bath all put together," says Sergio. He can't wait to come back.

His teacher asks,
"Did you have fun?"

"YES!"

"Great, next time we'll swim
without the floaties!"

Sergio will have to think about that . . .

For Jennifer and Sofia

Little, Brown and Company

Hachette Book Group USA
237 Park Avenue, New York, NY 10017
Visit our Web site at www.lb-kids.com

First Edition: May 2008

Library of Congress Cataloging-in-Publication Data

Rodriguez, Edel.
Sergio makes a splash / by Edel Rodriguez. — 1st ed.
p. cm.
Summary: Even though he loves water, Sergio the penguin is afraid to swim
in the deep water until he learns how.
ISBN 978-0-316-06616-7 (alk. paper)
[1. Penguins—Fiction. 2. Swimming—Fiction. 3. Fear—Fiction.] I. Title.
PZ7.L5346Se 2008
[E]—dc22
2007031076

10 9 8 7 6 5 4 3 2 1   SC   Manufactured in China

The illustrations in this book were created with oil-based woodblock ink
printed on paper, combined with digital media.